STAR OVER BETHLEHEM

and other stories

STAR OVER BETHLEHEM

and other stories
by
Agatha Christie Mallowan

Decorations by
Elsie Wrigley

DODD, MEAD & COMPANY, INC.

New York

For Hydie

Contents

A Greeting

Praise to the Yule Log!
    Leap, Flames, merrily.
Hail to the Wassail Bowl!
    Bubble, Wine, rosily!

In the Manger lies the Child;
Asses, Oxen, braying, lowing,
Cackling Hens and Cocks a'crowing.
Overfull the Inn to-night,
Up above a star shines bright,
Shepherds kneel beside their fold,
Wise Men bring their gifts of Gold,
Angels in the Sky above
Trumpet forth God's gift of Love.

Waken, children, one and all,
Wake to hear the trumpet call,
Leave your sleeping, 'tis the Day,
    Christmas, glorious Christmas Day!

Star over Bethlehem

Agatha Christie Mallowan

Mary looked down at the baby in the manger. She was alone in the stable except for the animals. As she smiled down at the child her heart was full of pride and happiness.

Then suddenly she heard the rustling of wings and turning, she saw a great Angel standing in the doorway.

The Angel shone with the radiance of the morning sun, and the beauty of his face was so great that Mary's eyes were dazzled and she had to turn aside her head.

Then the Angel said (and his voice was like a golden trumpet):

"Do not be afraid, Mary. . . ."

And Mary answered in her sweet low voice:

"I am not afraid, Oh Holy One of God, but the Light of your Countenance dazzles me."

The Angel said: "I have come to speak to you."

Mary said: "Speak on, Holy One. Let me hear the commands of the Lord God."

The Angel said: "I have come with no commands. But since you are specially dear to God, it is permitted that, with my aid, you should look into the future. . . ."

Then Mary looked down at the child and asked eagerly: "Into *his* future?"

Her face lit up with joyful anticipation.

" Yes," said the Angel gently. " Into *his* future . . . Give me your hand."

Mary stretched out her hand and took that of the Angel. It was like touching flame—yet flame that did not burn. She shrank back a little and the Angel said again:

" Do not be afraid. I am immortal and you are mortal, but my touch shall not hurt you. . . ."

Then the Angel stretched out his great golden wing over the sleeping child and said:

" Look into the future, Mother, and see your Son. . . ."

And Mary looked straight ahead of her and the stable walls melted and dissolved and she was looking into a Garden. It was night and there were stars overhead and a man was kneeling, praying.

Something stirred in Mary's heart, and her motherhood told her that it was her son who knelt there. She said thankfully to herself: " He has become a good man—a devout man—he prays to God." And then suddenly she caught her breath, for the man had raised his face and she saw the agony on it—the despair and the sorrow . . . and she knew that she was looking on greater anguish than any she had ever known or seen. For the man was utterly alone. He was praying to God, praying that this cup of anguish might be taken from him—and there was no answer to his prayer. God was absent and silent. . . .

And Mary cried out:

" Why does not God answer him and give him comfort? "

And she heard the voice of the Angel say:

" It is not God's purpose that he should have comfort."

Then Mary bowed her head meekly and said: " It is not for us to know the inscrutable purposes of God. But has this man —my son—has he no friends? No kindly human friends? "

The Angel rustled his wing and the picture dissolved into another part of the Garden and Mary saw some men lying asleep.

She said bitterly: " He needs them—my son needs them— and they do not care! "

The Angel said: " They are only fallible human creatures . . ."

Mary murmured to herself: " But he is a *good* man, my son. A good and upright man."

Then again the wing of the Angel rustled, and Mary saw a road winding up a hill, and three men on it carrying crosses, and a crowd behind them and some Roman soldiers.

The Angel said: " What do you see now? "

Mary said: " I see three criminals going to execution."

The left hand man turned his head and Mary saw a cruel crafty face, a low bestial type—and she drew back a little.

" Yes," she said, " they are criminals."

Then the man in the centre stumbled and nearly fell, and as he turned his face, Mary recognised him and she cried out sharply:

[12]

" No, no, it cannot be that my son is a *criminal*! "

But the Angel rustled his wing and she saw the three crosses set up, and the figure hanging in agony on the centre one was the man she knew to be her son. His cracked lips parted and she heard the words that came from them:

" *My God, my God, why hast thou forsaken me?* "

And Mary cried out: " No, no, it is not true! He cannot have done anything really wrong. There has been some dreadful mistake. It can happen sometimes. There has been some confusion of identity; he has been mistaken for someone else. He is suffering for someone else's crime."

But again the Angel rustled his wings and this time Mary was looking at the figure of the man she revered most on earth—the High Priest of her Church. He was a noble-looking man, and he stood up now and with solemn hands he tore and rent the garment he was wearing, and cried out in a loud voice:

" This man has spoken Blasphemy! "

And Mary looked beyond him and saw the figure of the man who had spoken Blasphemy—and it was her son.

Then the pictures faded and there was only the mudbrick wall of the stable, and Mary was trembling and crying out brokenly:

" I cannot believe it—I *cannot* believe it. We are a God-fearing straight-living family—all my family. Yes, and Joseph's family too. And we shall bring him up carefully to practise religion and to revere and honour the faith of his fathers. A son of ours could never be guilty of blasphemy—I cannot believe it! All this that you have shown me cannot be true."

Then the Angel said: " Look at me, Mary."

And Mary looked at him and saw the radiance surrounding him and the beauty of his Face.

And the Angel said: " What I have shown you is Truth. For I am the Morning Angel, and the Light of the Morning is Truth. Do you believe now? "

And sorely against her will, Mary knew that what she had been shown was indeed Truth . . . and she could not disbelieve any more.

The tears raced down her cheeks and she bent over the child in the manger, her arms outspread as though to protect him. She cried out:

" My child . . . my little helpless child . . . what can I do to save you? To spare you from what is to come? Not only from the sorrow and the pain, but from the evil that will blossom in your heart? Oh indeed it would have been better for you if you had never been born, or if you had died with your first breath. For then you would have gone back to God pure and unsoiled."

And the Angel said: " That is why I have come to you, Mary."

Mary said: " What do you mean? "

The Angel answered: " You have seen the future. It is in your power to say if your child shall live or die."

Then Mary bent her head, and amidst stifled sobs she murmured:

" The Lord gave him to me . . . If the Lord now takes him away, then I see that it may indeed be mercy, and though it tears my flesh I submit to God's will."

But the Angel said softly:

" It is not quite like that. God lays no command on you. The choice is *yours*. You have seen the future. Choose now if the child shall live or die."

Then Mary was silent for a little while. She was a woman who thought slowly. She looked once at the Angel for guidance, but the Angel gave her none. He was golden and beautiful and infinitely remote.

She thought of the pictures that had been shown her—of the agony in the garden, of the shameful death, of a man who, at the hour of death, was forsaken of God, and she heard again the dreadful word *Blasphemy*. . . .

And now, at this moment, the sleeping babe was pure and innocent and happy. . . .

But she did not decide at once, she went on thinking—going over and over again those pictures she had been shown. And in doing so a curious thing happened, for she remembered little things that she had not been aware of seeing at the time. She saw, for instance, the face of the man on the right-hand cross. . . . Not an evil face, only a weak one—and it was turned towards the centre cross and on it was an expression of love and trust and adoration. . . . And it came to Mary, with sudden wonder—" It was at *my son* he was looking like that . . ."

And suddenly, sharply and clearly, she saw her son's face as it had been when he looked down at his sleeping friends in the garden. There was sadness there, and pity and understanding and a great love . . . And she thought: " It is the face of a *good* man . . ." And she saw again the scene of accusation. But this time she looked, not at the splendid High Priest, but at the face of the accused man . . . and in his eyes was no consciousness of guilt. . . .

And Mary's face grew very troubled.

Then the Angel said:

" Have you made your choice, Mary? Will you spare your son suffering and evildoing?"

[15]

And Mary said slowly:

" It is not for me, an ignorant and simple woman, to understand the High Purposes of God. The Lord gave me my child. If the Lord takes him away, then that is His will. But since God has given him life, it is not for me to take that life away. For it may be that in my child's life there are things that I do not properly understand . . . It may be that I have seen only *part* of a picture, not the whole. My baby's life is his own, not mine, and I have no right to dispose of it."

" Think again," said the Angel. " Will you not lay your child in my arms and I will bear him back to God? "

" Take him in your arms if it is God's command," said Mary. " But *I* will not lay him there."

There was a great rustling of wings and a blaze of light and the Angel vanished.

Joseph came in a moment later and Mary told him of what had occurred. Joseph approved of what Mary had done.

" You did right, wife," he said. " And who knows, this may have been a lying Angel."

" No," said Mary. " He did not lie."

She was sure of that with every instinct in her.

" I do not believe a word of it all," said Joseph stoutly. "We will bring our son up very carefully and give him good religious instruction, for it is education that counts. He shall work in the shop and go with us to the Synagogue on the Sabbath and keep all the Feasts and the Purifications."

Looking in the manger, he said:

" See, our son is smiling . . ."

And indeed the boy was smiling and holding out tiny hands to his mother as though to say " Well Done."

But aloft in the vaults of blue, the Angel was quivering with pride and rage.

"To think that I should fail with a foolish, ignorant, woman! Well, there will come another chance. One day when *He* is weary and hungry and weak . . . Then I will take him up to the top of a mountain and show him the Kingdoms of this World of mine. I will offer him the Lordship of them all. He shall control Cities and Kings and Peoples . . . He shall have the Power of causing wars to cease and hunger and oppression to vanish. One gesture of worship to me and he shall be able to establish peace and plenty, contentment and good will—know himself to be a Supreme Power for Good. He can never withstand *that* temptation!"

And Lucifer, Son of the Morning, laughed aloud in ignorance and arrogance and flashed through the sky like a burning streak of fire down to the nethermost depths. . . .

In the East, three Watchers of the Heavens came to their Masters and said:

"We have seen a Great Light in the Sky. It must be that some great Personage is born."

But whilst all muttered and exclaimed of Signs and Portents a very old Watcher murmured:

"A Sign from God? God has no need of Signs and Wonders. It is more likely to be a Sign from Satan. It is in my mind that if God were to come amongst us, he would come very quietly. . . ."

But in the Stable there was much fun and good company. The ass brayed, and the horses neighed and the oxen lowed, and men and women crowded in to see the baby and passed him from one to the other, and he laughed and crowed and smiled at them all.

"See," they cried. "He loves everybody! There never was such a Child. . . ."

A Wreath for Christmas

When Mary made a Holly wreath
The blood ran red—ran red.
Another Mary wove the Thorns
That crowned her Master's head.
But the Mistletoe was far away
Across a Western sea,
And the Mistletoe was wreathed around
A Pagan Apple Tree.

In Glastonbury grew a Thorn,
When Joseph came to trade.
And the Holly Bush was common growth
In every wooded glade.
But the Mistletoe was sacred where
The Sun arose each morn,
And the Mistletoe knew nothing of
The Babe in Bethlehem born.

Saint Patrick sailed the stormy seas
To preach the Cross—and so
He found Eve's Tree—with serpent coiled—
And hung with Mistletoe.
" I bid thee, Serpent, leave this Land,
And open, Plant, thine ears."

He preached the Tale of Christ—and Lo!
The Mistletoe wept tears. . . .

The Holly bush has berries red,
Blood-red upon each bough.
The Thorn it blooms with golden flowers,
And Kissing's fashion now.
What will *you* give to Christ the Lord?
O! Pagan Bough so green?
" *The Tears that I have shed for One*
Whom I have never seen . . ."

Let Man then give his life for Man,
The blood-red berries say,
And Men have love for fellow men,
Where Gorse flowers bloom so gay.
And the Tears of Man be shed for Man
Where Mistletoe gleams white.
Come, pity, love and sacrifice. . . .
God bless us all this night!

The Naughty Donkey

Once upon a time there was a very naughty little donkey. He *liked* being naughty. When anything was put on his back he kicked it off, and he ran after people trying to bite them. His master couldn't do anything with him, so he sold him to another master, and that master couldn't do anything with him and also sold him, and finally he was sold for a few pence to a dreadful old man who bought old worn-out donkeys and killed them by overwork and ill treatment. But the naughty donkey chased the old man and bit him, and then ran away kicking up his heels. He didn't mean to be caught again so he joined a caravan that was going along the road. "Nobody will know who I belong to in all this crowd," thought the donkey.

These people were all going up to the city of Bethlehem, and when they got there they went into a big *Khan* full of people and animals.

The little donkey slipped into a nice cool stable where there was an ox and a camel. The camel was very haughty, like all camels, because camels think that they alone know the hundredth and secret name of God. He was too proud to speak to the donkey So the donkey began to boast. He loved boasting.

"I am a very unusual donkey," he said, " I have foresight *and* hindsight."

" What is that? " said the ox.

" Like my forelegs—in front of me—and my hind legs—behind me. Why, my great great, thirty-seventh time great grandmother belonged to the Prophet Balaam, and saw with her own eyes the Angel of the Lord! "

But the ox went on chewing and the camel remained proud.

Then a man and a woman came in, and there was a lot of fuss, but the donkey soon found out that there was nothing to fuss about, only a woman going to have a baby which happens every day. And after the baby was born some shepherds came and made a fuss of the baby—but shepherds are very simple folk.

But then some men in long rich robes came.

" V.I.P.s," hissed the camel.

" What's that? " asked the donkey.

" Very Important People," said the camel, " bringing gifts."

The donkey thought the gifts might be something good to eat, so when it was dark he began nosing around. But the first gift was yellow and hard, with no taste, the second made the donkey sneeze and when he licked the third, the taste was nasty and bitter.

" What stupid gifts," said the donkey, disappointed. But as he stood there by the Manger, the baby stretched out his little hand and caught hold of the donkey's ear, clutching it tight as very young babies will.

And than a very odd thing happened. The donkey didn't want to be naughty any more. For the first time in his life he wanted to be good. And *he* wanted to give the baby a gift—but he hadn't anything to give. The baby seemed to like his ear, but the ear was part of *him*—and then another strange idea came to him. Perhaps he could give the baby *himself*. . . .

It was not very long after that that Joseph came in with a tall stranger. The stranger was speaking urgently to Joseph, and as the donkey stared at them he could hardly believe his eyes!

The stranger seemed to dissolve and in his place stood an Angel of the Lord, a golden figure with wings. But after a moment the Angel changed back again into a mere man.

" Dear dear, I'm seeing things," said the donkey to himself. " It must be all that fodder I ate."

Joseph spoke to Mary.

" We must take the child and flee. There is no time to be lost." His eye fell on the donkey. " We will take this donkey here, and leave money for his owner whoever he may be. In that way no time will be lost."

So they went out on the road from Bethlehem. But as they came to a narrow place, the Angel of the Lord appeared with a flaming sword, and the donkey turned aside and began to climb the hillside. Joseph tried to turn him back on to the road, but Mary said:

"Let him be. Remember the Prophet Balaam."

And just as they got to the shelter of some olive trees, the

soldiers of King Herod came clattering down the road with drawn swords.

"Just like my great grandmother," said the donkey, very pleased with himself. "I wonder if I have foresight as well."

He blinked his eyes—and he saw a dim picture—a donkey fallen into a pit and a man helping to pull it out. . . . "Why, it's my Master, grown up to be a man," said the donkey. Then he saw another picture . . . the same man, riding on a donkey into a city. . . . " Of course," said the donkey. " He's going to be crowned King! "

But the Crown seemed to be, not Gold, but Thorns (the donkey loved thorns and thistles—but it seemed the wrong thing for a Crown) and there was a smell he knew and feared— the smell of blood; and there was something on a sponge, bitter like the myrrh he had tasted in the stable. . . .

And the little donkey knew suddenly that he didn't want foresight any more. He just wanted to live for the day, to love his little Master and be loved by him, and to carry Him and his mother safely to Egypt.

Gold, Frankincense and Myrrh

Gold, frankincense and myrrh. . . . As Mary stands
Beside the Cross, those are the words that beat
Upon her brain, and make her clench her hands,
On Calvary, in noonday's burning heat.
Gold, frankincense and myrrh. The Magi kneel
By simple shepherds all agog with joy,
And Angels praising God who doth reveal,
His love for men in Christ, the new born Boy.

Where now the incense? Where the kingly gold?
For Jesus only bitter myrrh and woe.
No kingly figure hangs here—just a son
In pain and dying. . . . How shall Mary know
That with his sigh " 'Tis finished," all is told;
Then—in *that* moment—Christ's reign has begun?

The Water Bus

Mrs Hargreaves didn't like people.

She tried to, because she was a woman of high principle and a religious woman, and she knew very well that one ought to love one's fellow creatures. But she didn't find it easy—and sometimes she found it downright impossible.

All that she could do was, as you might say, to go through the motions. She sent cheques for a little more than she could afford to reputable charities. She sat on committees for worthy objects, and even attended public meetings for abolishing injustices, which was really more effort than anything else, because, of course, it meant close proximity to human bodies, and she hated to be touched. She was able easily to obey the admonitions posted up in public transport, such as: " Don't travel in the rush hour "; because to go in trains and buses, enveloped tightly in a sweltering crowd of humanity, was definitely her idea of hell on earth.

If children fell down in the street, she always picked them up and bought them sweets or small toys to " make them better." She sent books and flowers to sick people in Hospital.

Her largest subscriptions were to communities of nuns in Africa, because they and the people to whom they ministered, were so far away that she would never have to come in contact with them, and also because she admired and envied the nuns who actually seemed to *enjoy* the work they did, and because she wished with all her heart that she were like them.

She was willing to be just, kind, fair, and charitable to people, so long as she did not have to see, hear or touch them.

But she knew very well that that was not enough.

Mrs Hargreaves was a middle-aged widow with a son and daughter who were both married and lived far away, and she herself lived in a flat in comfortable circumstances in London— and she didn't like people and there didn't seem to be anything she could do about it.

She was standing on this particular morning by her daily woman who was sitting sobbing on a chair in the kitchen and mopping her eyes.

"——never told me nothing, she didn't—not her own Mum! Just goes off to this awful place—and how she heard about it, I don't know—and this wicked woman did things to her, and it went septic—or what ever they call it—and they took her off to Hospital and she's lying there now, *dying* . . . Won't say who the man was—not even now. Terrible it is, my own daughter—such a pretty little girl she used to be, lovely curls. I used to dress her ever so nice. Everybody said she was a lovely little thing . . ."

She gave a gulp and blew her nose.

Mrs Hargreaves stood there wanting to be kind, but not really knowing how, because she couldn't really *feel* the right kind of feeling.

She made a soothing sort of noise, and said that she was very very sorry. And was there anything she could do?

Mrs Chubb paid no attention to this query.

" I s'pose I ought to have looked after her better . . . been at home more in the evenings . . found out what she was up to and who her friends were—but children don't like you poking your nose into their affairs nowadays—and I wanted to make a bit of extra money, too. Not for myself—I'd been thinking of getting Edie a slap-up gramophone—ever so musical she is—or something nice for the home. I'm not one for spending money on *myself* . . ."

She broke off for another good blow.

" If there is anything I can do ? " repeated Mrs Hargreaves. She suggested hopefully " A private room in the Hospital? "

But Mrs Chubb was not attracted by that idea.

" Very kind of you, Madam, but they look after her very well in the ward. And it's more cheerful for her. She wouldn't like to be cooped away in a room by herself. In the ward, you see, there's always something going on."

Yes, Mrs Hargreaves saw it all clearly in her mind's eye. Lots of women sitting up in bed, or lying with closed eyes; old women smelling of sickness and old age—the smell of poverty and disease percolating through the clean impersonal odour of disinfectants. Nurses scurrying along, with trays of instruments and trolleys of meals, or washing apparatus, and finally the screens going up round a bed . . . The whole picture made her shiver—but she perceived quite clearly that to Mrs Chubb's daughter there would be solace and distraction in " the ward " because Mrs Chubb's daughter liked people.

Mrs Hargreaves stood there by the sobbing mother and longed for the gift she hadn't got. What she wanted was to be able to put her arm round the weeping woman's shoulder and say something completely fatuous like " There, there, my dear "—and *mean it*. But going through the motions would be no good at all. Actions without feeling were useless. They were without content . . .

Quite suddenly Mrs Chubb gave her nose a final trumpet-like blow and sat up.

"There," she said brightly. "I feel better.

She straightened a scarf on her shoulders and looked up at Mrs Hargreaves with a sudden and astonishing cheerfulness.

"Nothing like a good cry, is there?"

Mrs Hargreaves had never had a good cry. Her griefs had always been inward and dark. She didn't quite know what to say.

"Does you good talking about things," said Mrs Chubb. "I'd best get on with the washing up. We're nearly out of tea and butter, by the way. I'll have to run round to the shops."

Mrs Hargreaves said quickly that she would do the washing up and would also do the shopping and she urged Mrs Chubb to go home in a taxi.

Mrs Chubb said no point in a taxi when the 11 bus got you there just as quick; so Mrs Hargreaves gave her two pound notes and said perhaps she would like to take her daughter something in Hospital? Mrs Chubb thanked her and went.

Mrs Hargreaves went to the sink and knew that once again she had done the wrong thing. Mrs Chubb would have much preferred to clink about in the sink, retailing fresh bits of information of a *macabre* character from time to time, and then she could have gone to the shops and met plenty of her fellow kind and talked to *them*, and *they* would have had relatives in hospitals, too, and they all could have exchanged stories. In that way the time until Hospital visiting hours would have passed quickly and pleasantly.

"Why do I always do the wrong thing?" thought Mrs Hargreaves, washing up deftly and competently; and had no need to search for the answer. "*Because I don't care for people.*"

When she had stacked everything away, Mrs Hargreaves took a shopping bag and went to shop. It was Friday and therefore a busy day. There was a crowd in the butcher's shop. Women pressed against Mrs Hargreaves, elbowed her aside, pushed baskets and bags between her and the counter. Mrs Hargreaves always gave way.

"Excuse me, *I* was here before you." A tall thin olive-skinned woman infiltrated herself. It was quite untrue and they both knew it, but Mrs Hargreaves stood politely back. Unfortunately, she acquired a defender, one of those large brawny women who are public spirited and insist on seeing justice is done.

"You didn't ought to let her push you around, luv," she admonished, leaning heavily on Mrs Hargreaves' shoulder and breathing gusts of strong peppermint in her face. "You was here long before she was. I come in right on her heels and I know. Go on now." She administered a fierce dig in the ribs. "Push in there and stand up for your rights!"

"It really doesn't matter," said Mrs Hargreaves. "I'm not in a hurry."

Her attitude pleased nobody.

The original thruster, now in negotiation for a pound and a half of frying steak, turned and gave battle in a whining slightly foreign voice.

"If you think you get here before me, why not you say? No good being so high and mighty and saying " (she mimicked the words) " *it doesn't matter*! How do you think that makes *me* feel? *I* don't want to go out of my turn."

"Oh no," said Mrs Hargreaves' champion with heavy irony. "Oh no, of course not! We all know that, don't we?"

She looked round and immediately obtained a chorus of assent. The thruster seemed to be well known.

"We know her and her ways," said one woman darkly.

"Pound and a half of rump," said the butcher thrusting

forth a parcel. " Now then, come along, who's next, please ? "

Mrs Hargreaves made her purchases and escaped to the street, thinking how really awful people were!

She went into the greengrocer next, to buy lemons and a lettuce. The woman at the greengrocer's was, as usual, affectionate.

" Well, ducks, what can we do for you to-day ? " She rang up the cash register; said " Ta " and " Here you are, dearie," as she pressed a bulging bag into the arms of an elderly gentleman who looked at her in disgust and alarm.

" She always calls me that," the old gentleman confided gloomily when the woman had gone in search of lemons. " ' Dear,' and ' Dearie ' and ' Love.' I don't even know the woman's name ! "

Mrs Hargreaves said she thought it was just a fashion. The old gentleman looked dubious and moved off, leaving Mrs Hargreaves feeling faintly cheered by the discovery of a fellow sufferer.

Her shopping bag was quite heavy by now, so she thought she would take a bus home. There were three or four people waiting at the bus stop, and an ill-tempered conductress shouted at the passengers.

" Come along now, hurry along, please—we can't wait here all day." She scooped up an elderly arthritic lady and thrust her staggering into the bus where someone caught her and steered her to a seat, and seized Mrs Hargreaves by the arm above the elbow with iron fingers, causing her acute pain.

" Inside, only. Full up now." She tugged violently at a bell, the bus shot forward and Mrs Hargreaves collapsed on top of a large woman occupying, through no fault of her own, a good three-quarters of a seat for two.

" I'm so sorry," gasped Mrs Hargreaves.

" Plenty of room for a little one," said the large woman cheerfully, doing her best without success to make herself smaller. " Nasty temper some of these girls have, haven't they? I prefer the black men myself. Nice and polite *they* are—don't hustle you. Help you in and out quite carefully."

She breathed good temper and onions impartially over Mrs Hargreaves.

" I don't want any remarks from you, thank you," said the bus conductress who was now collecting fares. " I'd have you know we've got our schedule to keep."

" That's why the bus was idling alongside the curb at the last stop but one," said the large woman. " Fourpenny, please."

Mrs Hargreaves arrived home exhausted by recrimination and unwanted affection, and also suffering from a bruised arm. The flat seemed peaceful and she sank down gratefully.

Almost immediately however, one of the porters arrived to clean the windows and followed her round telling her about his wife's mother's gastric ulcer.

Mrs Hargreaves picked up her handbag and went out again. She wanted—badly—a desert island. Since a desert island was not immediately obtainable—(indeed, it would probably entail a visit to a travel agency, a passport office, vaccination, possibly a foreign visa to be obtained and many other human contacts)—she strolled down to the river.

" A water bus," she thought hopefully.

There were such things, she believed. Hadn't she read about them? And there was a pier—a little way along the Embankment; she had seen people coming off it. Of course, perhaps a water bus would be just as crowded as anything else . . .

But here she was in luck. The steamer, or water bus, or whatever it was, was singularly empty. Mrs Hargreaves bought a ticket to Greenwich. It was the slack time of day and it was not a particularly nice day, the wind being distinctly chilly, so few people were on the water for pleasure.

There were some children in the stern of the boat with a weary adult in charge, and a couple of nondescript men, and an old woman in rusty black. In the bow of the boat there was only a solitary man; so Mrs Hargreaves went up to the bow, as far from the noisy children as possible.

The boat drew away from the pier out into the Thames. It was peaceful here on the water. Mrs Hargreaves felt soothed and serene for the first time today. She had got away from— from *what* exactly? " Away from it all! " that was the phrase, but she didn't know exactly what it meant. . . .

She looked gratefully around her. Blessed, blessed water.

So—so *insulating*. Boats plied their way up and down stream, but they had nothing to do with *her*. People on land were busy with their own affairs. Let them be—she hoped they enjoyed themselves. Here she was in a boat, being carried down the river towards the sea.

There were stops, people got off, people got on. The boat resumed its course. At the Tower of London the noisy children got off. Mrs Hargreaves hoped amiably that they would enjoy the Tower of London.

Now they had passed through the Docks. Her feeling of happiness and serenity grew stronger. The eight or nine people still on board were all huddled together in the stern—out of the wind, she supposed. For the first time she paid a little more attention to her fellow traveller in the bows. An Oriental of some kind, she thought vaguely. He was wearing a long cape-like coat of some woollen material. An Arab, perhaps? Or a Berber? Not an Indian.

What beautiful material the cloth of his coat was. It seemed to be woven all in one piece. So finely woven, too. She obeyed an almost irresistible impulse to touch it. . . .

She could never recapture afterwards the feeling that the touch of the coat brought her. It was quite indescribable. It was like what happens when you shake a kaleidoscope. The parts of it are the same parts, but they are arranged differently; they are arranged in a new pattern. . . .

She had wanted when she got on the water bus to escape from herself and the pattern of her morning. She had not escaped in the way she had meant to escape. She was still herself and she was still in the pattern, going through it all over again in her mind. But it was different this time. It was a different pattern because *she* was different.

[37]

She was standing again by Mrs Chubb—poor Mrs Chubb—She heard the story again only this time it was a different story. It was not so much what Mrs Chubb said, but what she had been feeling—her despair and—yes, her guilt. Because, of course, she was secretly blaming herself, striving to tell herself how she had done everything for her girl—her lovely little girl—recalling the frocks she had bought her and the sweets—and how she had given in to her when she wanted things—she had gone out to work, too—but of course, in her innermost mind, Mrs Chubb knew that it was not a gramophone for Edie she had been working for, but a washing machine—a washing machine like Mrs Peters had down the road (and so stuck up about it, too!). It was her own fierce housepride that had set her fingers to toil. True, she had given Edie things all her life—plenty of them—but had she *thought* about Edie enough? Thought about the boy friends she was making? Thought about asking her friends to the house—seeing if there wasn't some kind of party at home Edie could have? Thinking about Edie's character, her life, what would be best for her? Trying to find out more about Edie because after all, Edie was *her* business—the real paramount business of her life. And she mustn't be stupid about it! Good will wasn't enough. One had to manage not to be stupid, too.

In fancy, Mrs Hargreaves' arm went round Mrs Chubb's shoulder. She thought with affection: " You poor stupid dear. It's not as bad as you think. *I* don't believe she's dying at all." Of course Mrs Chubb had exaggerated, had sought deliberately for tragedy, because that was the way Mrs Chubb saw life—in melodramatic terms. It made life less drab, easier to live. Mrs Hargreaves understood so well. . . .

Other people came into Mrs Hargreaves' mind. Those women enjoying their fight at the butcher's counter. Characters, all of them. Fun, really! Especially the big red-faced woman with her passion for justice. She really liked a good row!

Why on earth, Mrs Hargreaves wondered, had she minded the woman at the greengrocer's calling her " Luv "? It was a kindly term.

That bad-tempered bus conductress—why—her mind probed, came up with a solution. Her young man had stood her up the evening before. And so she hated everybody, hated her monotonous life, wanted to make other people feel her power—one could so easily feel like that if things went wrong . . .

The kaleidoscope shook—changed. She was no longer *looking* at it—she was inside it—*part of it* . . .

The boat hooted. She sighed, moved, opened her eyes. They had come at last to Greenwich.

Mrs Hargreaves went back by train from Greenwich. The train, at this time of day, the lunch hour, was almost empty.

But Mrs. Hargreaves wouldn't have cared if it had been full . . .

Because, for a brief space of time, she was at one with her fellow beings. *She liked people.* Almost—she loved them!

It wouldn't last, of course. She knew that. A complete change of character was not within the bounds of reality. But she was deeply, humbly, and comprehendingly grateful for what she had been given.

She knew now what the thing that she had coveted was like. She knew the warmth of it, and the happiness—knew it, not from intelligent observation from without, but from within. From *feeling* it.

And perhaps, knowing now just what it was, she could learn the beginning of the road to it. . .?

She thought of the coat woven in the harmony of one piece. She had not been able to see the man's face. But she thought she knew who He was . . .

Already the warmth and the vision were fading. But she would not forget—she would never forget!

"Thank you," said Mrs Hargreaves, speaking from the depths of a grateful heart.

She said it aloud in the empty railway carriage.

The mate of the water bus was staring at the tickets in his hand.

"Where's t'other one?" he asked.

"Whatchermean?" said the Captain who was preparing to go ashore for lunch.

"Must be someone on board still. Eight passengers there was. I counted them. And I've only got seven tickets here."

"Nobody left on board. Look for yourself. One of 'em must have got off without your noticing 'im—either that or he walked on the water!"

And the Captain laughed heartily at his own joke.

In the Cool of the Evening

The church was fairly full. Evensong, nowadays, was always better attended than morning service.

Mrs Grierson and her husband knelt side by side in the fifth pew on the pulpit side. Mrs Grierson knelt decorously, her elegant back curved. A conventional worshipper, one would have said, breathing a mild and temperate prayer.

But there was nothing mild about Janet Grierson's petition. It sped upwards into space on wings of fire.

" God, help him! Have mercy upon him. Have mercy upon *me*. Cure him, Lord. Thou hast all power. Have mercy—have mercy. Stretch out Thy hand. Open his mind. He's such a sweet boy—so gentle—so innocent. Let him be healed. Let him be *normal*. Hear me, Lord. Hear me . . . Ask of me anything you like, but stretch out Thy hand and make him whole. Oh God, *hear* me. *Hear* me. With Thee all things are possible. My faith shall make him whole— I *have* faith—I believe. I *believe*! Help me! "

The people stood. Mrs Grierson stood with them. Elegant, fashionable, composed. The service proceeded.

The Rector mounted the steps of the pulpit, gave out his text.

Part of the 95th psalm; the tenth verse. Part of the psalm

we sing every Sunday morning. "It is a people who do err in their hearts, for they have not known my ways."

The Rector was a good man, but not an eloquent one. He strove to give to his listeners the thought that the words had conveyed to him. A people that erred, not in what they *did*, not in *actions* displeasing to God, not in overt sin—but a people not even knowing that they erred. A people who, quite simply, did not know God ... They did not know what God was, what he wanted, how he showed himself. They could know. That was the point the Rector was striving to make. Ignorance is no defence. They *could* know.

He turned to the East.

"And now to God the Father ..."

He'd put it very badly, the Rector thought sadly. He hadn't made his meaning clear at all ...

Quite a good congregation this evening. How many of them, he wondered, really *knew* God?

Again Janet Grierson knelt and prayed with fervour and desperation. It was a matter of will, of concentration. If she could get through—God was all powerful. If she could reach him ...

For a moment she felt she was getting there—and then there was the irritating rustle of people rising; sighs, movements. Her husband touched her arm. Unwillingly she rose. Her face was very pale. Her husband looked at her with a slight frown. He was a quiet man who disliked intensity of any kind.

In the porch friends met them.

"What an attractive hat, Janet. It's new, isn't it?"

"Oh no, it's terribly old."

"Hats are so difficult," Mrs Stewart complained. "One hardly ever wears one in the country and then on Sunday

[42]

one feels odd. Janet, do you know Mrs Lamphrey—Mrs
Grierson. Major Grierson. The Lamphreys have taken Island
Lodge."

"I'm so glad," said Janet, shaking hands. "It's a delightful
house."

"Everyone says we'll be flooded out in winter," said Mrs
Lamphrey ruefully.

"Oh no—not *most* years."

"But *some* years? I knew it! But the children were mad
about it. And of course they'd adore a flood."

"How many have you?"

"Two boys and a girl."

"Edward is just the same age as our Johnnie," said Mrs
Stewart. "I suppose he'll be going to his public school next
year. Johnnie's going to Winchester."

"Oh, Edward is much too much of a moron ever to pass
common entrance, I'm sure," sighed Mrs Lamphrey. "He

doesn't care for anything but games. We'll have to send him to a crammer's. Isn't it terrible, Mrs Grierson, when one's children turn out to be morons?"

Almost at once, she felt the chill. A quick change of subject—the forthcoming fête at Wellsly Park.

As the groups moved off in varying directions, Mrs Stewart said to her friend:

"Darling, I ought to have warned you!"

"Did I say something wrong? I thought so—but what?"

"The Griersons. Their boy. They've only got one. And *he's* subnormal. Mentally retarded."

"Oh how awful—but I couldn't know. Why does one always go and put one's foot straight into things?"

"It's just that Janet's rather sensitive . . ."

As they walked along the field path, Rodney Grierson said gently,

"They didn't mean anything. That woman didn't know."

"No. No, of course she didn't."

"Janet, can't you try——"

"Try what?"

"Try not to mind so much. Can't you accept——"

Her voice interrupted him, it was high and strained.

"No, I can't *accept*—as you put it. There must be *something* that could be done! He's physically so perfect. It must be just some gland—some perfectly simple thing. Doctors will find out some day. There must be something—injections—hypnotism."

"You only torture yourself, Janet. All these doctors you drag him round to. It worries the boy."

"I'm not like you, Rodney. I don't give up. I prayed *again* in church just now."

"You pray too much."

"How can one pray 'too much'? I believe in God, I tell you. I *believe* in him. I have faith—and faith can move mountains."

"You can't give God orders, Janet."

"What an extraordinary thing to say!"

"Well——" Major Grierson shifted uncomfortably.

"I don't think you know what faith is."

"It ought to be the same as trust."

Janet Grierson was not listening.

"To-day—in church, I had a terrible feeling. I felt that God wasn't there. I didn't feel that there was no God—just that He was somewhere else . . . But where?"

"Really, Janet!"

"Where could He be? Where could I find Him?"

She calmed herself with an effort as they turned in at the gate of their own house. A stocky middle-aged woman came out smiling to meet them.

"Have a nice service? Supper's almost ready. Ten minutes?"

"Oh good. Thank you, Gertrude. Where's Alan?"

"He's out in the garden as usual. I'll call him."

She cupped her mouth with her hands.

"A—lan. A—lan."

Suddenly, with a rush, a boy came running. He was fair and blue-eyed. He looked excited and happy.

"Daddy—Mummy—look what I've found."

He parted his cupped hands carefully, showing the small creature they contained.

"Ugh, horrible." Janet Grierson turned away with a shudder.

"Don't you like him? Daddy!" He turned to his father.

"See, he's partly like a frog—but he isn't a frog—he's got

[45]

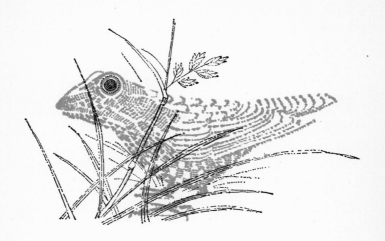

feathers and a sort of wings. He's quite new—not like any other animal."

He came nearer, and dropped his voice.

"I've got a name for him. I call him Raphion. Do you think it's a nice name?"

"Very nice, my boy," said his father with a slight effort. The boy put the strange creature down.

"Hop away, Raphion, or fly if you can. There he goes. He isn't afraid of me."

"Come and get ready for supper, Alan," said his mother.

"Oh yes, I'm hungry."

"What have you been doing?"

"Oh, I've been down at the end of the garden, talking to a friend. He helps me name the animals. We have such fun."

"He's happy, Janet," said Grierson as the boy ran up the stairs.

"I know. But what's going to become of him? And those

horrible things he finds. They're all about everywhere now-adays since the accident at the Research station."

"They'll die out, dear. Mutations usually do."

"Queer heads—and extra legs!" She shuddered.

"Well, think of all the legs centipedes have. You don't mind them?"

"They're natural."

"Perhaps everything has to have a first time."

Alan came running down the stairs again.

"Have you had a nice time? Where did you go? To church?" He laughed, trying the word out. "Church—church—that's a funny name."

"It means God's house," said his mother.

"Does it? I didn't know God lived in a house."

"God is in Heaven, dear. Up in the sky. I told you."

"But not always? Doesn't He come down and walk about? In the evenings? In summer? When it's nice and cool?"

"In the Garden of Eden," said Grierson, smiling.

"No, in this garden, here. He'd like all the funny new animals and things like I do."

Janet winced.

"Those funny animals—darling." She paused. "There was an accident, you know. At the big Station up on the downs. That's why there are so many of these queer—things about. They get born like that. It's very sad!"

"Why? I think it's exciting! Lots of new kinds of things being born all the time. I have to find names for them. Sometimes I think of lovely names."

He wriggled off his chair.

"I've finished. Please—can I go now? My friend is waiting for me in the garden."

His father nodded. Gertrude said softly.

" All children are the same. They always invent a ' friend '
to play with."

" At five, perhaps. Not when they're thirteen," said Janet
bitterly.

" Try not to mind, dear," said Gertrude gently.

" How can I help it ? "

" You may be looking at it all the wrong way."

Down at the bottom of the garden, where it was cool under
the trees, Alan found his friend waiting.

He was stroking a rabbit who was not quite a rabbit but
something rather different.

" Do you like him, Alan ? "

" Oh yes. What shall we call him ? "

" It's for you to say."

" Is it really ? I shall call him—I shall call him—Forteor. Is
that a good name ? "

" All your names are good names."

" Have you got a name yourself? "

" I have a great many names."

" Is one of them God ? "

" Yes."

" I thought it was ! You don't really live in that stone house
in the village with the long thing sticking up, do you ? "

" I live in many places . . . But sometimes, in the cool of
the evening, I walk in a garden—with a friend and talk about
the New World——"

Jenny by the Sky

Come down to me, Jenny, come down from the hill
Come down to me here where I wait
Come down to my arms, to my lips, my desire
Come down all my hunger to sate

But Jenny walks lonely, her head in the air,
She walks on the hill top, the wind in her hair,
She will not come down to me, loud though I cry
She walks with the wind, upturned face to the sky . . .

In the cool of the evening I walked in the glade,
And there I met God . . . and I was not afraid.
Together we walked in the depths of the wood
And together we looked at the things we had made
Together we looked—and we saw they were good . . .

God made the World and the stars set on high
The Galaxies rushing, none knows where or why.
God fashioned the Cosmos, the Universe wide,
And the hills and the valleys, the birds in the wood
God made them and loved them, and saw they were good . . .

And I—have made Jenny! To walk on the hill.
She will not come down to me loud though I cry;
She walks there for ever, her face to the sky,

She will not come down though I call her,
She will not come down to my greed,
She is as I dreamed her . . . and made her
Of my loving and longing and need . . .

With my mind and my heart I made Jenny,
I made her of love and desire,
I made her to walk on the hill top
In loneliness, beauty and fire. . . .

In the cool of the evening I walked in the wood
And God walked beside me. . . .
We both understood.

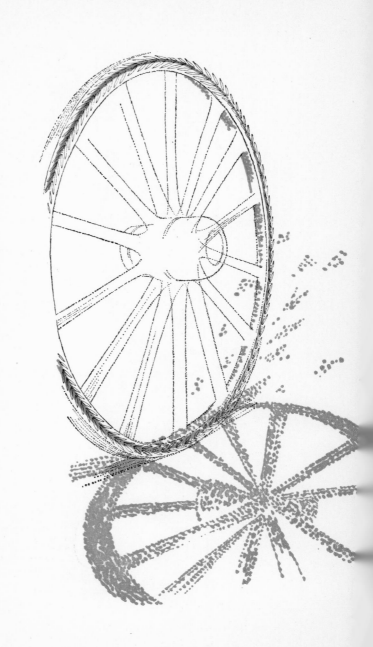

Promotion in the Highest

They were walking down the hill from the little stone church on the hillside.

It was very early in the morning, the hour just before dawn. There was no one about to see them as they went through the village, though one or two sleepers sighed and stirred in their sleep. The only human being who saw them that morning was Jacob Narracott, as he grunted and sat up in the ditch. He had collapsed there soon after he came out of the Bel and Dragon last night.

He sat up and rubbed his eyes, not quite believing what he saw. He staggered to his feet and shambled off in the direction of his cottage, made uneasy by the trick his eyes had played him. At the crossroads he met George Palk, the village constable, on his beat.

"You'm late getting home, Jacob. Or should I say early?" Palk grinned.

Jacob groaned, and rocked his head in his hands.

"Government's been and done something to the beer," he affirmed. "Meddling again. I never used to feel like this."

"What'll your Missus say when she sees you rolling home at this hour?"

"Won't say anything. She's away to her sister's."

" So you took the opportunity to see the New Year in ? "

Jacob grunted. Then he said uneasily: " You seen a lot of people just now, George? Coming along the road? "

" No. What sort of people ? "

" Funny people. Dressed odd."

" You mean Beats ? "

" Nah, not Beats. Sort of old-fashioned like. Carrying things, some of 'em was."

" What sort of things ? "

" Ruddy great wheel, one had—a woman. And there was a man with a gridiron. And one rather nice looking wench, dressed very rich and fancy with a great big basket of roses."

" Roses? This time of year? Was it a sort of procession ? "

" That's right. Lights on their heads they had, too."

" Aw, get on, Jacob! Seeing things—that's what's the matter with you. Get on home, put your head under the tap, and sleep it off."

" Funny thing is, I feel I've seen 'em before somewhere— but for the life of me I can't think where."

" Ban the bomb marchers, maybe."

" I tell you they was dressed all rich and funny. Fourteen of them there was. I counted. Walking in pairs mostly."

" Oh well, some New Year's Eve party coming home maybe: but if you ask me, I'd say you did yourself too well at the Bel and Dragon, and that accounts for it all."

" Saw the New Year in proper, we did," agreed Jacob. " Had to celebrate special, seeing as it wasn't only 'Out with the Old Year, and in with the New.' It's out with the old Century and in with the New one. January 1st, A.D. 2000, that's what to-day is."

" Ought to mean something," said Constable Palk.

"More compulsory evacuation, I suppose," grumbled Jacob. "A man's home's not his castle nowadays. It's out with him, and off to one of these ruddy new towns. Or bundle him off to New Zealand or Australia. Can't even have children now unless the Government says you may. Can't even dump things in your back garden without the ruddy Council coming round and saying its got to go to the village dump. What do they think a back garden's *for*? What it's come to is, nobody treats you like you were *human* any more...."

His voice rumbled away ...

"Happy New Year," Constable Palk called after him....

The Fourteen proceeded on their way.

St Catherine was trundling her Wheel in a disconsolate manner. She turned her head and spoke to St Lawrence who was examining his Gridiron.

"What can I *do* with this thing?" she asked.

"I suppose a wheel always comes in useful," said St Lawrence doubtfully.

"What for?"

"I see what you mean—it was meant for torture—for breaking a man's body."

"Broken on the wheel." St Catherine gave a little shudder. "What are you going to do with your gridiron?"

"I thought perhaps I might use it for cooking something."

"Pfui," said St Cristina as they passed a dead stoat.

St Elizabeth of Hungary handed her one of her roses.

St Cristina sniffed it gratefully. St Elizabeth fell back beside St Peter.

"I wonder why we all seem to have paired up," she said thoughtfully.

[55]

" Those do, perhaps, who have something in common," suggested Peter.

" Have we something in common? "

" Well, we're both of us liars," said Peter cheerfully.

In spite of a lie that would never be forgotten, Peter was a very honest man. He accepted the truth of himself.

" I know. I know! " Elizabeth cried. " I can't bear to remember. How could I have been so cowardly—so weak, that day? Why didn't I stand there bravely and say, " I am taking bread to the hungry? " Instead, my husband shouts at me, " What have you got in that basket? " And I shiver and stammer out " Nothing but roses . . ." And he snatched off the cover of the basket"—" And it *was* roses," said Peter gently.

" Yes. A miracle happened. Why did my Master do that for me? Why did he acquiesce in my lie? Why? Oh why? "

St Peter looked at her.

He said:

" So that you should never forget. So that pride could never lay hold of you. So that you should know that you were weak and not strong."

" I, too——" He stopped and then went on.

" I who was so sure that I could never deny him, so certain that I, above all the others, would be steadfast. I was the one who denied and spoke those lying cowardly words. Why did he choose *me*—a man like me? He founded his Church on me—Why? "

" That's easy," said Elizabeth. " Because you loved him. I think you loved him more than any of the others did."

" Yes, I loved him. I was one of the first to follow him. There was I, mending the nets, and I looked up, and there he was watching me. And he said, " Come with me." And I went. I think I loved him from the very first moment."

[56]

" You are so nice, Peter," said Elizabeth.

St Peter swung his keys doubtfully.

" I'm not sure about that Church I founded . . . It's not turned out at all as we meant . . ."

" Things never do. You know," Elizabeth went on thoughtfully. " I'm sorry now I put that leper in my husband's bed. It seemed at the time a fine defiant Act of Faith. But really— well, it wasn't very *kind*, was it? "

St Appolonia stopped suddenly in her tracks.

" I'm so sorry," she said. " I've dropped my tooth. That's the worst of having such a small emblem."

She called: " Anthony. Come and find it for me."

They were in the Land of the Saints now, and as they breathed its special fragrance St Cristina cried aloud in joy. The Holy Birds sang, and the Harps played.

But the Fourteen did not linger. They pressed forward to the Court of Assembly.

The Archangel Gabriel received them.

" The Court is in Session," he said. " Enter."

The Assembly Chamber was wide and lofty. The walls were made of mist and cloud.

The Recording Angel was writing in his Golden Book. He laid it aside, opened his Ledger and said, " Names and addresses, please."

They told him their names and gave their address. St Petrock-on-the-Hill. Stickle Buckland.

" Present your Petition," said the Recording Angel.

St Peter stepped forward.

" There is unrest amongst us. We ask to go back to Earth."

" Isn't Heaven good enough for you? " asked the Recording Angel. There was, perhaps, a slight tinge of sarcasm in his voice.

[57]

" It is too good for us."

The Recording Angel adjusted his Golden Wig, put on his Golden Spectacles, and looked over the top of them with disapprobation.

" Are you questioning the decision of your Creator? "

" We would not dare—but there was a ruling——"

The Archangel Gabriel, as Mediator and Intermediary between Heaven and Earth, rose.

" If I may submit a point of law? "

The Recording Angel inclined his head.

" It was laid down, by Divine decree, that in the Year A.D. 1000 and in every subsequent 1000th Year, there should be fresh Judgments and Decisions on such points as were brought to a special Court of Appeal. To-day is the Second Millennium. I submit that every person who has ever lived on earth has to-day a right of Appeal."

The Recording Angel opened a large Gold Tome and consulted it. Closing it again, he said:

" Set out your Case."

St Peter spoke.

" We died for our Faith. Died joyfully. We were rewarded. Rewarded far beyond our deserts. We—" he hesitated and turned to a young man with a beautiful face and burning eyes. " You explain."

" It was not enough," said the young man.

" Your reward was not enough? " The Recording Angel looked scandalised.

" Not our reward. Our service. To die for the Faith, to be a Saint, is not enough to merit Eternal Life. You know my story. I was rich. I obeyed the Law. I kept the commandments. It was not enough. I went to the Master. I said to him: " Master, what shall I do to inherit Eternal Life? "

"You were told what to do, and you did it," said the Recording Angel.

"It was not enough."

"You did more. After you had given all your possessions to the poor, you joined the disciples in their mission. You suffered Martyrdom. You were stoned to death in Ephesus."

"It was not enough."

"What more do you want to do?"

"We had Faith—burning Faith. We had the Faith that can move mountains. Two thousand years have taught us that we could have done more. We did not always have enough Compassion. . . ."

The word came from his lips like a breath from a summer sea. It whispered all round the Heavens. . . .

"This is our petition: Let us go back to Earth in Pity and Compassion to help those who need help."

There was a murmur of agreement from those around him.

The Recording Angel picked up the Golden Intercom on his desk. He spoke into it in a low murmur.

He listened. . . .

Then he spoke—briskly, and with authority.

"Promotion Granted," he said. "Approval in the Highest."

They turned to go, their faces radiant.

"Hand in your Crowns and Halos at the door, please."

They surrendered their Crowns and Halos and went out of the Court. St Thomas came back.

"Excuse me," he said politely. "But what you said just now—was it *Permission* Granted? Or was it *Promotion* Granted?"

"Promotion. After two thousand years of Sainthood, you are moving up to a higher rank."

"Thank you. I *thought* it was promotion you said. But I wanted to make *sure*."

He followed the others.

"He always had to make sure," said Gabriel. "You know—sometimes—I can't help wondering what it would be like to have an immortal soul. . . ."

The Recording Angel looked horrified.

"Do be careful, Gabriel. You know what happened to Lucifer."

"Sometimes I can't help feeling a little sorry for Lucifer. Having to rank below Adam upset him terribly. Adam wasn't much, was he?"

"A poor type," agreed the Recording Angel. "But he and all his descendants were created in the image of God with immortal souls. They *have* to rank above the Angels."

"I've often thought Adam's soul must have been a very small one."

"There has to be a beginning for everything," the Recording Angel pointed out severely.

Mrs Badstock heaved and pulled. The smell of the village dump was not agreeable. It was an unsightly mass of old tyres, broken chairs, ragged quilts, old kerosene tins, and broken bedsteads. All the things that nobody could possibly want. But Mrs Badstock was tugging hopefully. If that old pram was anyway repairable— She heaved again and it came free. . . .

"Drat!" said Mrs. Badstock. The upper portion of the pram was not too bad, but the wheels were missing.

She threw it down angrily.

"Can I help you?" A woman spoke out of the darkness.

"No good. Blasted thing's got no wheels."

" You want a wheel? I've got one here."

" Ta, ducks. But I need four. And anyway, yours is much too big."

" That's why I thought we could make it into four—with a little adjustment." The woman's fingers strayed over it pushing, pulling.

" There! How's that? "

" Well, I never! However did you— Now, if we'd got a nail or two—or a screw. I'll get my hubby——"

" I think I can manage." She bent over the pram. Mrs Badstock peered down to try and see what was happening.

The other woman straightened up suddenly. The pram stood on four wheels.

" It will want a little oil, and some new lining."

" I can see to that easy! *What* a boon it will be. You're quite a little home mechanic, aren't you, ducks? How on earth did you manage it? "

" I don't know really," said St Catherine vaguely. " It just —happens."

The tall woman in the brocade dress said with authority: " Bring them up to the house. There's plenty of room."

The man and the woman looked at her suspiciously. Their six children did the same.

" The Council are finding us somewhere," said the man sullenly.

" But they're going to separate us," said the woman.

" And you don't want that? "

" Of course we don't."

Three of the children began to cry.

" Shut your bloody mouths," said the man, but without rancour.

"Been saying they'd evict us for a long time," said the man. "Now they've done it. Always whining about their rent. I've better things to do with my money than pay rent. That's Councils all over for you."

He was not a nice man. His wife was not very nice either, St Barbara thought. But they loved their children.

"You'd better all come up to my place," she said.

"Where is it?"

"Up there." She pointed.

They turned to look.

"But—that's a *Castle*," the woman exclaimed in awestruck tones.

"Yes, it's a Castle all right. So you see, there will be lots of room. . . ."

St Scoithín stood rather doubtfully on the seashore. He wasn't quite sure what to do with his Salmon.

He could smoke it, of course—it would last longer that way. The trouble was that it was really only the rich who like smoked salmon, and the rich had quite enough things already. The poor much preferred their salmon in tins. Perhaps——

The Salmon writhed in his hands, and St Scoithín jumped.

"Master," said the Salmon.

St Scoithín looked at it.

"It is nearly a thousand years since I saw the sea," said the Salmon pleadingly.

St Scoithín smiled at him affectionately. He walked out on the sea, and lowered the Salmon gently into the water.

"Go with God," he said.

He walked back to the shore, and almost immediately

stumbled over a big heap of tins of salmon with a purple flower stuck on top of them.

St Cristina was walking along a crowded City street. The traffic roared past her. The air was full of diesel fumes.

"This is terrible," said St Cristina, holding her nose. "I must do something about this. And why don't they empty the dustbins oftener? It's very bad for people." She pondered. "Perhaps I had better go into Parliament. . . ."

St Peter was busy setting out his Loaf and Fish stall.

"Old Age Pensioners first," he said. "Come on, Grand-dad."

"Are you National Assistance?" the old man asked suspiciously.

"That kind of thing."

"Not religious, is it? I'm not going to sing hymns."

"When the food's all gone, I shall preach," said Peter. "But you don't have to stay on and listen."

"Sounds fair enough. What are you going to preach about?"

"Something quite simple. Just how to attain Eternal Life."

A younger man gave a hoot of laughter.

"Eternal Life! What a hope!"

"Yes," said Peter cheerfully, as he shovelled out parcels of hot fish. "It *is* a hope. Got to remember that. There's always Hope."

In the Church of St Petrock-on-the-Hill, the Vicar was sitting sadly in a pew, watching a confident young architect examining the old painted screen.

"Sorry, Vicar," said the young man, turning briskly.

" Not a hope in Hell, I'm afraid. Oh! sorry again. I oughtn't
to have put it like that. But it's long past restoring. Nothing
to be done. The wood's rotten, and there's hardly any paint
left—not enough to see what the original was like. What is it?
Fifteenth century?"

" Late fourteenth."

" What are they? Saints?"

" Yes. Seven each side." He recited. " St Lawrence, St
Thomas, St Andrew, St Anthony, St Peter, St Scoithín, and
one we don't know. The other side: St Barbara, St Catherine,
St Appolonia, St Elizabeth of Hungary, St Cristina the
Astonishing, St Margaret, and St Martha."

" You've got it all very pat."

" There were church records. Not in very good condition.
Some we had to make out by their emblems—St Barbara's
castle for instance, and St Lawrence's gridiron. The original
work was done by Brother Bernard of the Benedictines of
Froyle Abbey."

" Well, I'm sorry about my verdict. But everything has
got to go sometime. I hear your rich parishioner has offered
you a new screen with modern symbolical figures on it?"

" Yes," said the Vicar without enthusiasm.

" Seen the big new Cathedral Centre at New Huddersfield?
Coventry was good in its time, but this is streets ahead of it!
Takes a bit of getting used to, of course."

" I am sure it would."

" But it's taken on in a big way! Modern. Those old
Saints," he flicked a hand towards the screen. " I don't
suppose anyone knows who half of them are nowadays. I
certainly don't. Who was St Cristina the Astonishing?"

" Quite an interesting character. She had a very keen sense
of smell. At her funeral service the smell of her putrefying

body affected her so much that she levitated out of her coffin up to the roof of the Chapel."

"Whew! Some Saint! Oh well, it takes all sorts to make a world. Even your old Saints would be very different nowadays, I expect." . . .

The Saints of God

Saint Lawrence with his Gridiron
Saint Catherine with her Wheel
Saint Margaret with her Dragon
Saint Wilfred with his Seal

The Saints of God are marching
Are marching down the hill
The Saints of God are marching
To ascertain God's Will

" Oh, we have sat in Glory
And worn the Martyr's Crown
But we now make petition
That we from Heaven go down.

" In pity and compassion
Let us go back to men
And show them where the Pathway
Leads back to Heaven again. . . ."

The Island

There were hardly any trees on the island. It was arid land, an island of rock, and the goats could find little to eat. The shapes of the rocks were beautiful as they swept up from the sea, and their colour changed with the changing of the light, going from rose to apricot, to pale misty grey, deepening to mauve and to stern purple, and in a last fierceness to orange, as the sun sank into that sea so rightly called wine-dark. In the early mornings the sky was a pale proud blue, and seemed so high up and so far away that it filled one with awe to look up at it.

But the women of the island did not look up at it often, unless they were anxiously gazing for signs of a storm. They were women and they had to work. Since food was scarce, they worked hard and unceasingly, so that they and their children should live. The men went out daily in the fishing boats. The children herded the goats and played little games of their own with pebbles in the sun.

Today the women with great jars of fresh water on their heads, toiled up the slope from the spring in the cleft of the cliff, to the village above.

Mary was still strong, but she was not as young as most of the women, and it was an effort to her to keep pace with them.

To-day the women were very gay, for in a few days' time

there was to be a wedding. The girl children danced round their elders and chanted monotonously:

"I shall go to the wedding . . . I shall go to the wedding . . . I shall have a ribbon in my hair . . . I shall eat roseleaf jelly . . . roseleaf jelly in a spoon . . ."

The mothers laughed, and one child's mother said teasingly: "How do you know I shall take you to the wedding?"

Dismayed, the child stared.

"You *will* take me—you will—you *will* . . ." And she clung to Mary, demanding: "She will let me go to the wedding? Say she will!"

And Mary smiled and said gently: "I think she will, sweetheart!"

And all the women laughed gaily, for to-day they were all happy and excited because of the wedding.

"Have you ever been to a wedding, Mary?" the child asked.

"She went to her own," laughed one of the women.

"I didn't mean your own. I meant a wedding party, with dancing and sweet things to eat, and roseleaf jam, and honey?"

"Yes. I have been to weddings." Mary smiled, "I remember one wedding . . . very well . . . a long time ago."

"With roseleaf jam?"

"I think so—yes. And there was wine . . ."

Her voice trailed off as she remembered.

"And when the wine runs out, we have to drink water," one of the women said. "That always happens!"

"We did not drink water at this wedding!"

Mary's voice was strong and proud.

The other women looked at her. They knew that Mary had come here with her son from a long way away, and that she did not often speak of her life in earlier days, and that there was some very good reason for that. They were careful not to ask her questions, but of course there were rumours, and now suddenly one of the older children piped up and spoke like a parrot.

"They say you had a son who was a great criminal and was executed for his crimes. Is that true?"

The women tried to hush her down, but Mary spoke, her eyes looking straight ahead of her.

"Those that should know said he was a criminal."

"But you didn't think so?" the child persisted.

Mary said after a pause:

"I do not know of myself what is right or wrong. I am too ignorant. My son loved people—good and bad equally . . ."

They had reached the village now and they divided to go to their own homes. Mary had farthest to go, to a stone croft at the very end of the cluster of sprawling buildings.

"How is your son? Well, I hope?" asked one of the women politely.

"He is well, thanks be to God."

To erase the memory of what had been said before, the woman said kindly:

"You must be proud of this son of yours. We all know that he is a Holy Man. They say he has visions and walks with God."

"He is a good son," said Mary. "And, as you say, a very Holy Man."

She left them to go her own way and they stood looking after her for a moment or two.

"She is a good woman."

"Yes. It is not her fault, I am sure, that her other son went wrong."

[71]

"Such things happen. One does not know why. But she is lucky in this son. There are times when he is animated by the Spirit, and then he prophesies in a loud voice. His feet, they say, rise off the ground—and then he lies like one dead for a while."

They all nodded and clucked in wonder and pleasure to have such a holy man amongst them.

Mary went to the little stone cottage, and stood the jar of water down. She glanced towards where a man sat at a rudely-fashioned table. There was a scroll of parchment in front of him and he bent over it, writing with a pen, pausing now and then, whilst his eyes half closed, as he lost himself in the ardours of the spirit. . . .

Mary was careful not to disturb him. She busied herself in getting together the midday meal.

The man was a man of great beauty, though no longer young. He had great delicacy of feature, and the far-away eyes of a soul to whom spiritual life is as real as the life of the body. Presently his hand slackened on the pen, and he seemed almost to pass into a trance, neither moving nor speaking, and indeed hardly breathing.

Mary put the dishes on the table.

"Your meal is ready, my son."

As one who hears a faint sound from very far away, he shook his head impatiently.

"The vision . . . so near . . ." he muttered, "so near . . . When—oh when?"

"Come, my son, eat."

He waved the food away.

"There is another hunger, another thirst! The food of the spirit . . . The thirst for righteousness. . . ."

"But you must eat. To please me. To please your mother."

[72]

Gently she coaxed and scolded—and at last he came down from that high exaltation, and smiled at her with a human half-teasing look.

"Must I then eat to satisfy you?"

"Yes. Or else I shall be made unhappy."

So he ate to please her, hardly noticing what the food was.

Then he bethought himself to ask:

"How is it with you, dear mother? You have all you need?"

"I have all I need," said Mary.

He nodded, satisfied, and took up his pen once more.

When Mary had cleared all away, she went out and stood looking out over the sea.

Her hands clasped together, she bowed her head and spoke softly under her breath.

"Have I done all I could? I am such an ignorant woman. I do not always know how to serve and minister to one who is assuredly a Saint of God. I wash his linen, and prepare his food, and bring him fresh water, and wash his feet. But more than that I know not how to do."

As she stood there, her anxiety passed. Serenity came back to her worn face.

On the shore beneath, a boat had drawn into the little stone pier. It was not an ordinary fishing boat, but one that stood high in the water, and had a big curving prow of richly carved wood. Two men landed from it, and some old men who were mending fishing nets came to accost the strangers.

Politely the two men made known their business.

"We seek amongst the islands hereabouts for an island on which is said to dwell the Queen of Heaven."

The old fishermen shook their heads.

"What you seek is certainly not here. We have no shrine such as you describe."

"Perhaps your women have knowledge of such a shrine?" one of the strangers suggested. "Women are often secretive about such matters."

"Inquire if you wish. One of us will go up and show you the village."

The strangers went up with their guide. The women came clustering out of their houses. They were excited and interested, but they all shook their heads.

"No Goddess has her Shrine here, alas! Neither by our Spring nor elsewhere."

They told him of other shrines reported from other places, but none of them were what the strangers sought.

"But we have a Holy Man here," said one of the women proudly. "He is skin and bone, and fasts all the time when his old mother will let him."

But the strangers were not looking for a Holy Man however great his sanctity.

"At least inquire of him," one of the women insisted.
"He might know of such a thing as you seek."

So they went to the Holy Man's croft; but he was lost in
his Vision and for some time did not even hear what they
were saying to him.

Then he was angry and said:

"Do not go astray after heathen Goddesses. Not after the
Scarlet Woman of Babylon, nor after the Abominations of
the Phoenicians. There is only one Redeemer, and that is the
Living Son of God."

So the strangers went away, but the Holy Man's mother
ran secretly after them.

"Do not be angry," she begged. "My son was not meaning to be discourteous to you; but he is so pure and so holy
himself that he lives in a region far above this earth. He is
a good man and a good son to me."

The strangers spoke kindly to her.

"We are not offended. You are a good woman, and have
a good son."

"I am a very ordinary woman," she said. "But I must tell
you that you should not believe in all these Aphrodites and
Astartes and whatever their heathen names are. There is only
one God, our Father in Heaven."

"You say you are only an ordinary woman," said the older
of the two strangers. "But although your face is old and
ravaged with the lines of sorrow, yet to my mind you have a
face of great beauty—and I in my time was apprenticed to
a great sculptor, so I know what beauty is."

Mary, amazed, cried out: "Once, perhaps, when I wove
the coloured tapestry in the Temple, or when I poured my
husband's wine in the shop, and held my first-born son in my
arms. But *now*!"

But the old sculptor shook his head.

"Beauty lies beneath the skin," he insisted. "In the bone. Yes, and beneath that again—in the heart. So I say that you are a beautiful woman, perhaps more beautiful now than you were as a young girl. Farewell—and may you be blessed."

So the strangers rowed away in their boat, and Mary went slowly back to the croft and to her son.

The coming of the strangers had made him restless. He was walking up and down and his hands clasped his head in suffering.

Mary ran to him and held him in her arms.

"What is it, dear son?"

He groaned out: "The spirit has gone out of me . . . I am empty . . . empty . . . I am cut off from God—from the joy of his Presence."

Then she comforted him—as she had comforted him many times before, saying: "From time to time, this has to be—we do not know why. It is like the wave of the sea. It goes out from the shore, but it returns, my son, it returns."

But he cried out:

"You do not *know*. You cannot understand . . . You do not know what it is to be caught up in the Spirit, to be exalted with the great glory of God!"

And Mary said humbly:

"That is true. *That*, I have not felt. For me, there has been only memory . . ."

"Memory is not enough!"

But Mary said fiercely: "It is enough for me!"

And she went to the door and stood there, looking out over the sea where the strangers had gone away. . . .

As she stood there, she felt a strange expectancy rising in her; a fluttering hopeful joy. Almost, she went down to

[76]

the shore again, but she restrained herself, for she knew that her son would soon need her. And so it was. He began to shake all over, and his body jerked, and at last his limbs stiffened and he fell to the ground and lay like one dead. Then she covered him over for warmth and placed a fold of the cloak between his lips, in case the convulsions should come back. But he lay there motionless, and there was no sign, even, that he breathed.

Mary knew from experience that he would not stir for many hours, and she walked out again on to the hillside. It was growing dark now and the moon was rising over the sea.

Mary stood there savouring the welcome coolness of the evening. Her mind was full of memories of the past, of a hurried flight into Egypt, of the carpenter's shop, and of a marriage in Cana. . . .

And again that joyous expectancy rose in her.

"Perhaps," she thought, "perhaps at last the time has come."

Presently, very slowly, she began to walk down to the sea. . . .

The moon rose in the sky, and it made a silvery path across the water, and as the light grew stronger, Mary saw a boat approaching.

She thought: "The strangers are coming back again . . ."

But it was not the strangers . . . She could see now that it was not the handsome carved boat of the strangers. This was a rough fishing boat—the kind of boat that had been familiar to her all her life . . .

And then she knew—quite certainly. . . . It was *his* boat and he had come for her at last . . .

And now she ran, slipping and stumbling over the rough

stones of the beach. And as she reached the water's edge, half sobbing and half panting, she saw one of the three men step out of the boat onto the sea and walk along the moonlit path towards her.

Nearer and nearer he came . . . and then—and then . . . she was clasped in his arms . . . Words poured from her, incoherently, trying to tell so much.

" I have done as you asked me—I have looked after John— He has been as a son to me. I am not clever—I cannot always understand his high thoughts and his visions, but I have made him good food, and washed his feet, and tended him and loved him . . . I have been his mother and he has been my son. . . ? "

She looked anxiously up into his face, asking him a question.

" You have done all I asked you," he said gently. " Now— you are coming home with me."

" But how shall I get to the boat? "

" We will walk together on the water."

She peered out to sea.

" Are those—yes, they are—Simon and Andrew, are they not? "

" Yes, they wanted to come."

" How happy—Oh! how happy we are going to be," cried Mary. " Do you remember the day of the marriage in Cana. . .?"

And so, walking together on the water, she poured out to her son all the little events and happenings of her life, and even how two strangers had come that very day looking for the " Queen of Heaven." And how ridiculous it was!

" They were quite right," said her Son. " The Queen of Heaven was here on the island, but they did not know her when they saw her . . ."

And he looked into the worn, ravaged, beautiful face of his mother, and repeated softly:

"*No, they did not know her when they saw her!*"

In the morning, John awoke and rose from the ground.

It was the Lord's Day, and at once he knew that this was to be the great day of his life!

The Spirit rushed into him....

He took up his pen and wrote:

I saw a new heaven and a new earth ... And behind me I heard a great voice as of a trumpet ... Saying:

I am Alpha and Omega, the first and the last ... I am he that liveth and was dead; and behold, I am alive for evermore, Amen; and have the keys of hell and of death ... Behold, I come quickly; and my reward is with me, to give every man according as his work shall be ...